DON'T

LET THE

BEDBUGS

BITE.

By E.A. Green

Published By
Breaking Rules Publishing

Soft Cover – 10102
Published by Breaking Rules Publishing
St Petersburg, Florida
www.breakingrulespublishing.com

Every illustration within this storybook book came from the internet's free domain.

"If Any Copyrighted Material Was Accidently Used," It was done Unintentionally by this Author and Illustrator Who Is More Than Willing to Remove Them at the Owners Request.

The

Greenman's

Favorite

Bedtime Fables,

Fairy Tales

And

Nightmares.

I and the spirits of Gomez and Morticia,

Dedicate this Bedtime Storybook

To All of the Unnamed Wednesday's and Pugsley's

In Us Wanna-Be Addams's.

QUOTES FROM THE GREENMAN.
A FAIRIES TALE.

QUOTES FROM THE GREENMAN.
BLOODY MARY.

QUOTES FROM THE GREENMAN.
GORGE GEORGY.

QUOTES FROM THE GREENMAN.
MR. BLISTER.

QUOTES FROM THE GREENMAN.
HELLHOUND.

QUOTES FROM THE GREENMAN.
EDDIE BEAR.

QUOTES FROM THE GREENMAN.
MR. BOOGIE.

QUOTES FROM THE GREENMAN.
LITTLE LIZZY.

QUOTES FROM THE GREENMAN.

QUOTES FROM THE GREENMAN.

The Future is not set in stone

Until we take that last breath

And close the book.

"SO,"

Turn the page

And

Read On.

A FAIRIE'S TALE.

If the animals are whispering

As flowers do hush,

Voice not to speak

And turn from thus.

If forest gleam

At pitch black hour,

Sparkling and Twinkling

Despite night's power.

And in the sun

Blind you be,

Drawing the strength

of will from thee.

Touch Not!

Go Not!

Turn Away!

The Fairies are never

There to play.

You see my friend

Their trap is set.

So mind your greed

And take not step.

For when they appear

And you are caught.

Your spirit will leave

This forest not.

And as a rule of Fairy Law,

A tree you'll be

For one and all.

So when you see

And your eyes do pleasure.

Remember.

It's Your Soul Fairies

Deem as Treasure.

QUOTES FROM THE GREENMAN.

Life is but the wind on an ever-changing surface.

A passing shadow in the structure of time.

Only to be remembered as Fables or Legends,

"To Future Generations,"

Which will only come to be recalled as dreams.

I wonder how they will remember you.

BLOODY MARY.

If you want

To scare your friends

And have a freaky time.

Go into

A darkened room

And say this creepy rhyme.

Here I stand

Between two mirrors

A candle will I light.

When I see

Her bloody face

I'll smash my head

Into that place.

All these things

Will You do

After You've rhymed this

Three Times Through.

Bloody Mary.

Bloody Mary.

Lite the candle bright.

Spin around.

Don't look down.

You'll miss a Frightful Site.

Bloody Mary.

Bloody Mary.

The candle must still burn

Spin around.

Don't Look Down.

It's just your second turn.

Bloody Mary.

Bloody Mary.

Dim the candle low

Spin around.

Don't Look Down.

She's about to show.

Bloody Mary.

Bloody Mary.

Now that you've done three

Spin around.

Don't Look Down.

Onward we must be.

Now smash your head

Into the place

Where she reflects back

On Your Face.

Bloody Mary.

Bloody Mary.

Listen to her glee.

Spin around.

Don't Look Down.

Your Bloody Dead

Like She.

QUOTES FROM THE GREENMAN.

If You want to make an evil demon jiggle;

Pull his tale

Slap his horns

And give his chin a tickle.

I'm Sure To Bet

By the time your through

His fanged sharped lips will wiggle too.

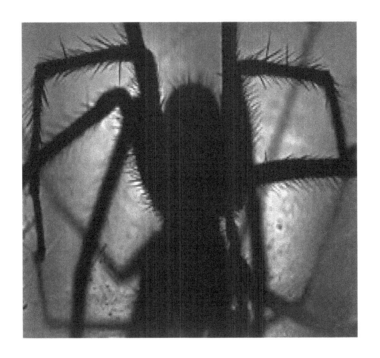

GORGE GEORGY

Mommy say's

It's beddy-bye time.

So, everyone sing

His deadly rhyme.

Now lay down

Your sleepy head.

So, Gorge Georgy

Thinks you're dead.

Cause if You Don't

And He sees You peepin.

The hairy little critter

Will come along creepin.

So, cover your head

Or dinner You'll be.

He Laughs Out Loud

HEE. HEE. HEE.

Gorge Georgy

Ribbons and bows.

He loves to chew

On sweet girls toes.

You will know

When He's around.

They'll be all wet

And slimy dark brown.

So, don't be scared

When Georgy's a nippin.

Or, He'll bite off your toes

While his tongue as a lickin.

So, cover your head

Or dinner You'll be.

He Laughs Out loud

HEE. HEE. HEE.

Now onward with

George's nursery rhyme.

He's deadly hungry

And You're Tasting So Fine.

Gorge Georgy

Dollies and tea.

For You He Is Coming

That's his giggling glee.

Your fingers are next

Maybe, you'll keep them.

Clicking sounds do scare him

Better start snappin.

And if you can

Send him away.

Switch rooms with your brother

Before that next day.

The eight-legged critter

Is coming back you see.

His hunger still burns

And he needs to feed.

So, cover your head

Or dinner You'll be.

He Laughs Out Loud

HEE. HEE. HEE.

Gorge Georgy

Boys are toads.

The slimy tad poles

Have smelly green toes.

He's said to profess

That those are the best.

While dribble drooling

For a taste of grotesque.

So, wash your hands

And both your feet too.

Before getting in bed

Or, He'll eat on you.

The hairs on his legs

Will prick up and swell.

Saying supper is ready

They can tell by the smell.

So, cover your head

Or dinner You'll be.

He Laughs Out Loud

HEE. HEE. HEE.

If his legs do skitter

Across the wood floor.

He's coming for You

From his home closet door.

So, if You value your life

And you'd like to keep tickin.

You better stay still

While Georgy's a lickin.

Because if you don't

And he starts to nibble.

Your fingers and toes

Will no longer tickle.

So, cover your head

Or dinner You'll be.

He Laughs Out Loud

HEE. HEE. HEE.

Gorge Georgy

Chocolate and cream.

God how he loves

To make little kids Scream.

I can still hear his laugh

I can still feel his fangs

I can still see his many eyes

Looking right into me.

So, check your toes

And fingers too.

When the sun does rise

After his nightly boo.

And if they're not there

And not Loudly clickin.

Gorge Georgy

Was the one nippin.

For the night is His

The day time too.

If your digits are missin

Georgy spider found you.

So, cover your head

Or dinner You'll be.

He Laughs Out Loud

HEE. HEE. HEE.

QUOTES FROM THE GREENMAN.

To make a sad clown happy

"You Must First,"

Turn his frown upside down.

So, cut off his face,

Then spin it around.

Now you have

a smiley clown

Who's no longer sad

Who's no longer down.

MR. BLISTER.

When you wake up

And find there are sores

You now have a new friend

Who's much to abhor.

It's called a little bedbug

And It is here to stay

And they never will ever go away.

He's the little vampire

Who hides during the day

Just waiting for your sleepy head

To lay back down his way.

It waits until it's dark

When you're no longer waken

Then creeps under the sheets

A slurp of You It's drinking.

And if your slimy ooze

Reminds It of bacon

Every last drop It's thinking of taking.

He's the little vampire

Who hides during the day

Waiting for your sleepy head

To lay back down his way.

Mr. Blister is Its name

And feeding on people

Is his nightly fame.

And He's chosen You

For His next dinner date

So, remember these rules

Or You'll be on His plate.

He's the little vampire

Who hides during the day

Waiting for your sleepy head

To lay back down his way.

You better look good

Before crawling under the covers

Checking those edges beyond all the others.

Because if you miss one

Or even just two

They are all going to feed

On every inch of you.

He's the little vampire

Who hides during the day

Waiting for your sleepy head

To lay back down his way.

QUOTES FROM THE GREENMAN.

Kitchen Witchin is part of the baking process.

So, you better get out of Grandma's way

Or she'll chop you right up

Mix your meat in

And serve you as pie

To her tea party friends.

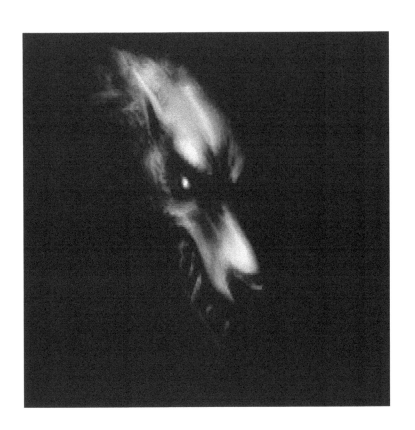

HELLHOUND.

If you are on

The out and go.

The night has fallen

His howls do blow.

You better run

And find a place.

Before He smells

Your scared fears face.

So, try not to cry

Or give yourself up.

Because, He Most Certainly

Will eat You for Sup.

If the moon is full

Young and bright.

You'll certainly find

A Werewolf Fright.

He's out on the prowl

Hunting for food.

Looking and sniffing

For fresh meat like You.

So, try not to cry

Or give yourself up.

Because, He Most Certainly

Will eat You for Sup.

As he gets

To where you do hide.

His nose does a sniffle

Because your fear ripples.

So, what to no end

Are you gonna do.

As his whiskers rub by

And tickles times two.

So, try not to cry

Or give yourself up.

Because, He Most Certainly,

Will eat You for Sup.

The best advice

I give to a single.

Is Don't go outside

When funny bone jingles.

Or, You'll end up fleeing

As tears do dribble.

Hoping you're not

His bloody next nibble.

So, try not to cry,

Or give yourself up.

Because, He Most Certainly

Will eat You for Sup.

The hounds of hell

Most Certainly Will.

Chew your bones

From their meat filled pate.

The next time you

Stroll alone.

On a quiet moonlit

Hellhound date.

So, try not to cry

Or give yourself up.

Because, He Most Certainly,

Will eat You for Sup.

I didn't listen

To my own words.

When the laughy bone

Rang and Ringled.

Now I'm sliding

Down It's throat.

My dying Screams

Just dwindle.

So, try not to cry

Or give yourself up.

Because He Most Certainly

Will eat You for Sup.

The next time his night

Does call out to you.

Remember these things

Long, Hard and Through.

The hairy big beast

Mr. Werewolf by name.

Will use Your Bones

To clean his plate.

So, try not to cry,

Or give yourself up.

Because, He Most Certainly

Will eat You for Sup.

QUOTES FROM THE GREENMAN.

If the Boogeyman comes a knockin

And you don't ask him what for?

He'll kick down the door

And stroll right on in

So, Always Lock It Before.

EDDIE BEAR.

Once upon a time; every child had an Eddie Bear to love, watch over and protect them. They could always be seen running, playing and chasing the children they so loved and adored.

Some of them even wore cloths and shoes like a real kid.

Eddie bears sat at the table, ate with their families and slept snuggle in the beds of every household member.

And that was because everyone had to have their own personal bear.

But, not every boy and girl cared for their Eddie bears.

"Those Eddie Bears who just happened to be the unlucky ones," were beaten, starved and abused by their protectors.

Many of them had been tortured and ripped apart by the hands of those that professed to care them. While some of the Eddie

Bears had an ear or two missing; others had their eyes plucked out and an arm or leg ripped off.

There were even those that had been purposely disfigured by knives, scissors and fire.

Not everyone loved their Eddie bears like they should have.

And that's when it happened.

One day an Eddie Bear could no longer take the horrors that were being bestowed upon it, and Savagely Attacked the child that was dragging it through the mud before trying to drown it in the bathtub.

When word got out that, "once again," someone had tried to kill an Eddie bear; the other abused bears, "and those that were not," rose up and attacked their protectors, captors and killers.

The people were so shocked that such a docile creature could do such a thing; that a decree was sent out to the masses. Every last Eddie Bear must be hunted down, killed and destroyed.

Even their pelts must be burned.

There could be no trace, "what so ever," of their existence.

And so the people did.

Well, almost everyone.

A few of the doll makers decided to create an Eddie bear version and, "unbeknownst to everyone else," used their pelts for the coverings. And that's why, "as of today," some children pass away in their sleep.

They don't have a Teddy bear in their rooms.

They Have An Eddie Bear!

Because so many Teddy bears were made; the Eddie Bears quickly disappeared into the masses that were bought and purchased for baby's, children and even some adults.

No one, "other than their makers," had any idea that the possessed Eddie Bears were seeking revenge on those that had killed them and their kind. And that's because their creators where, "accidently," killed just days after bringing them, "Somehow?" back to life.

That's why You should always Treat Your Bear Right.

"You never know," your Teddy bear could actually be an Eddie bear.

So, if you're in bed and hear a noise in your bedroom; make sure that, "before going to sleep," you have a Teddy bear and not an Eddie bear. Because, "if you do," they will hunt down anyone who hurts, mistreats or maims them.

That's why You should Always Love and Respect Your Bear.

QUOTES FROM THE GREENMAN.

If a Monster comes a creepin

Grab your baseball bat and ball.

They've always got time

To stop and play

Before they eat you all.

MR. BOOGIE.

He's the little centipede

Who lives under your bed.

At night he likes to stay real warm

While sleeping in your head.

So, what can you do

To hold him at bay.

But keep those eye's opened

So He'll stay away.

But first he must crawl

Across the place where you sleep.

He's going for his snuggly bed

By starting at your feet.

So, what can you do

To hold him at bay.

But keep those eye's opened

So He'll stay away.

The jittery little bug

Who dances like the devil.

Has a thousand tapping legs

And loves to cause trouble.

So, what can you do

To hold him at bay.

But keep those eye's opened

So He'll stay away.

His pointy sharpened feet

As he goes up your leg.

Will cause you to scream Real Loud

While he happily comes your way.

So, what can you do

To hold him at bay.

But keep those eye's opened

So He'll stay away.

Mr. Boogie's on your back

Your neck is in his view.

Once he reaches that sweet, sweet spot

Your ear will feel him too.

So, what can you do

To hold him at bay.

But keep those eye's opened

So He'll stay away.

It's almost that time

To crawl into bed.

He just has to get

Through the hole in your head.

So, what can you do

To hold him at bay.

But keep those eye's opened

So He'll go away.

Now he's inside

Warm, safe and gowned.

He's tucked into bed

And sleeping so sound.

So, what can you do

To hold him at bay.

But keep those eyes opened

So He'll go away.

QUOTES FROM THE GREENMAN.

If a zombie ask you for a bite to eat,

You better give him a finger.

Oh, Silly Me.

Zombies never ask for just one bite,

They always ask for two.

LITTLE LIZZY.

If Mommy wants to talk with her friends

And sends you outside to play.

There is a new kid in town

who lives on your block.

And, she's just a hop, skip and jump; away.

Little Lizzy is her name

And she just has, one favorite game.

It's called swing the bloody ax

And see your family run.

Doesn't that sound

Oh, So Fun.

She tried playing it with her dad

But he was too tired and that made her mad.

So, Little Lizzy swung anyway

Ending his nap

As his life drained away.

After knocking him down

A bloody notch of Ew.

She then asked her mom

To play the game too.

It was then Lizzy realized

She was no longer blue.

While swinging the ax

Forty times through.

As she sat all alone

Pondering her slaughter.

Your knock on the door

Made her thoughts ponder.

Who can that be

She shakingly said.

It's your next-door neighbor

And his name is Ed.

And there shyly standing

On her front porch stoop.

Stood a new friend to be

Of unfortunate fate.

For you are now Lizzy's,

chosen play date.

For she needed a friend

A boy should do.

So, that is why

She bloody picked you.

The smile on her face

Said all that was needed.

As you walked right in

And quietly pleaded.

Do you want to play

And be my friend.

I'll be yours

To the very end.

And quicker than her ax,

slammed into Daddy's head.

I most certainly do

She happily said.

Just stay right here

while I say goodbye.

To those that are still dying

and whining inside.

After kissing her parents

Pulling the ax from the dead.

Lizzy ran outside

Sending shivers of dread.

Her bloody new ax

With its fresh sharpened edge.

Was hungry for more

She Laughingly said.

Let's go to your house

Are your parents' home now.

I'd bet they'd so love

To see the girlfriend you've found.

Cause if we're best friends

As so you have said.

You'll swing my ax too

Until they are quite dead.

Now we both shall see

Lizzy giggles with glee.

As she knocks on their door

Yelling ring-a-ling ding.

She's looking at you

To tie up the score.

While your Mommy and Daddy

Stand in Abhor.

Because that's what best friends

Are Bloody made for.

Lizzy's Favorite game

You both now shall play.

If not for tomorrow

It will so be today.

Now swing her Bloody ax

And see your family run.

Doesn't that sound

Oh, So Fun.

QUOTES FROM THE GREENMAN.

Never ask a spirit to cross their fingers

And solemnly swear.

They Can't.

Their Ghost!

CPSIA information can be obtained
at www.ICGtesting.com
Printed in the USA
LVHW010035250222
711932LV00003B/574